Happy Birthday, Puppy Pals!

ADAPTED BY **MICHAEL OLSON**

BASED ON THE EPISODE WRITTEN BY **JESSICA CARLETON**

FOR THE SERIES CREATED BY **HARLAND WILLIAMS**

ILLUSTRATED BY THE **DISNEY STORYBOOK ART TEAM**

DISNEP PRESS

Los Angeles · New York

Today is a pawtastic day!

The sun is shining, the birds are singing, and it's time for Bob to wake up! "Hooray! It's our birthday today!" Rolly shouts, bouncing on Bob's bed.

"I love birthdays," Bingo says, "and I especially love our birthday!"

"Happy birthday, fellas!" Bob says with a yawn. "It's pretty early. Why don't you play until I get out of bed?"

The pups give Bob one more lick and then head for the yard. It's going to be the best puppy birthday ever!

Rolly heads straight for his favorite thing in the backyard: his stick collection. He finds a new stick and proudly adds it to the pile.

CRASH!

The new stick makes the pile fall over. "I wish my sticks would stop spilling everywhere," Rolly says with a sigh. "It would be great to have something to put them in."

Bingo plays his favorite game: launching his Captain Dog action figure.

BOING!

Captain Dog flies out of the launcher!

Bingo tries launching Captain Dog again. **SNAP!**

The spring on the launcher breaks.
"Oh, no!" Bingo cries.

After the backyard disasters, Bingo and Rolly go inside for breakfast.

"So, what did you get each other for gifts?" Hissy asks her little brothers. The pups look at Hissy, confused. "Don't you want to give each other something special?" Hissy asks.

"I want you to have the best birthday ever, Rolly!" Bingo says.
"Ditto!" says Rolly.

"C'mon, Rolly. We've got a birthday gift mission!" Bingo says. "I'm going to find you a present."

"And I'm going to find *you* a present!" Rolly replies.

MISSION: GET A PAWSOME GIFT FOR MY BROTHER

Bingo runs and finds the perfect gift—a stick from Rolly's collection. Hissy smiles. "Why don't you think of something Rolly doesn't have?" she suggests.

Then Bingo remembers what Rolly said earlier. "A stick holder!" he shouts.

Rolly finds a gift, too—Bingo's ball. "Okay, but what would Bingo like that he doesn't have already?" Hissy asks.

"He liked launching his Captain Dog toy," Rolly says. "I'll look for something springy!"

Bingo spots Cupcake and Rufus playing with a box that would
be perfect for Rolly's stick collection. "Could I have that box for
Rolly?" he asks.

"Not unless you can trade it for something better," Cupcake says.
Bingo comes up with a plan.

When Rolly goes to see his friend Dallie, he sees a spring holding up his doghouse door.

"That spring is just what I've been looking for!" Rolly exclaims.

"Well, I need it to keep my door open," Dallie says, "but if you have something else that'll work, I'm happy to trade."

"I'll be back!" Rolly shouts, running for home.

Rolly trades his stick collection for Dallie's spring. "I'll miss you all," he says, taking one last look at his collection.

"Seems like you really love those sticks," says Dallie.

"Yeah," Rolly says, "but not as much as I love my brother! See ya! I've got a present to wrap."

Meanwhile, Bingo takes all his favorite toys to Cupcake and
Rufus to make a trade. Cupcake spots Bingo's Captain Dog action
figure. "That's the one I want!"

"Okay," Bingo says with a sigh. "For Rolly, I'll trade."

The pups meet in the center of the yard with their gifts.
"Open yours first!" shouts Bingo.

"No, you go first!" Rolly says excitedly.

They decide to open them at the same time. Bingo opens his gift.
"It's a spring to launch your Captain Dog action figure!"
Rolly explains.

"And yours is a holder for your stick collection!"
Bingo tells Rolly.

"What are you waiting for?" Bingo asks. "Put your sticks in there!"

"I can't," Rolly says. "I traded my stick collection to Dallie for that spring. So let's launch Captain Dog!"

Bingo shrugs. "We can't. . . . I traded him to Cupcake for your present."

"Aw," Hissy says. "I feel bad that you can't play with your toys."

"Yeah," says Bingo. "But I have a brother who traded his favorite thing in the world just to make me happy."

"And that's better than any present I can think of," Rolly adds.

Just then, Bob calls the puppies into the house. "Who's ready for a birthday party?" he asks, presenting Bingo and Rolly with sweaters he knitted himself.

Hissy has presents for the puppies, too.

"My stick collection!" Rolly shouts.

"And my Captain Dog! How did you get our stuff back?" Bingo asks.

"Oh, I just made a couple of trades," Hissy explains.

The pups give her BIG hugs. "You're the best kitty sister in the whole wide world!" Rolly says.

"I know," Hissy says with a smile.